A FAKE FIANCÉ ON SNOW RIDGE

SNOW RIDGE SHIFTERS #2

L. E. WILSON

EVERBLOOD
PUBLISHING

ISBN: 978-1-945499-78-4

Print Edition

Publication Date: May 4, 2023

Proofreader: Mackenzie @ NiceGirlNaughtyEdits.com

Cover Design by Dar at WickedSmartDesigns.com

CHAPTER 1

ADAM

Adam tipped his beer up to his mouth and took a long drink as he watched Riko and Addison on the dance floor—if you could call a hastily cleared space in this run-down bar a "dance floor."

Addison was a natural, her body swaying effortlessly to the music. His friend, Riko, on the other hand, well...

Let's just say, dancing was never his forte.

However, as the new alpha of the Central Colorado Pack, Riko would excel. Adam had no doubts about that, and that's why he came with him without a second thought when Riko asked him and Lex to come back to Colorado to help him get this unruly bunch of wolves under control. Neither of them had held a very high position in their former pack, and so Keegan—the Oklahoma alpha—agreed to let them go, with the invitation to return if they ever wanted to. It made sense that Riko would want a couple of familiar faces around him. His old pack here in Colorado that he grew up with was practically all strangers to him now.

Adam had known Riko since he was just a kid and Riko was straight out of high school. That was when he'd shown up in Oklahoma and fought his way into the new pack. He was a good guy. Liked to stir the pot sometimes. But he had a good heart and he meant well. As alpha, he was always open to conversation and hearing what the rest of the pack had to say, but he also didn't take any shit.

Adam's eyes continued to wander around the old bar. If he had to guess, he'd say it was still the original structure that had been built when the town was first founded, and tonight it was packed full. He glanced down at the floor with concern as the old wood gave a bit with the weight of so many people walking over it. The entire fucking town must've squeezed in there to celebrate New Year's. Humans and wolves alike were drinking and carrying on like this was the first chance they'd gotten to leave their homes in a year. And maybe for some, it was. There wasn't a whole lot to do in this place. As a matter of fact, Greg's was the only bar in town.

A woman's voice cut through the general noise. That wouldn't normally catch his attention. Lots of ladies were letting their hair down and having a good 'ol time. But there was something that was a little too close to fear in her tone that had Adam searching for the owner of this particular voice. It only took him a second.

"Hell, Jeff. Let me get a drink first before you try to drag me out there."

His eyes landed on a young woman with loose, dark blonde curls beneath a red beanie, making her way toward the bar. Though she smiled at the folks she knew, her wide blue eyes, when they met his, screamed for help, and as she got closer, he could smell the acrid scent of fear on her. Adam shifted his glance to the much larger guy behind her, who was practically shoving people out of his way in an effort to keep up with her.

She rushed up beside Adam and threw her purse on the bar, then started shrugging out of her heavy coat, laying it over the back of the stool beside her. Beneath the fear, her scent hit him hard, catching him off guard for a second. It wasn't any kind of perfume. He didn't think she was wearing any. All he could smell was soap and shampoo and the natural earthy scent of her. But holy fuck, she smelled good. Like a summer day in the middle of winter. "Help me," she whispered with a smile that was clearly all for show.

A human man maybe wouldn't have heard her plea with all of the music and activity, but Adam heard her just fine, and he didn't hesitate. "Hey, babydoll," he greeted her. "'Bout time you got here." Throwing his arm over her shoulders, he turned his back on the dark-haired guy following her and flagged down his friend behind the bar. "Hey, Greg! A drink for..." he trailed off.

"Faye," she whispered.

"Faye," he finished.

"Thanks," she told him when Greg put a bottle of Bud Light down in front of her.

"Put it on my tab." Greg gave him a strange look but didn't say anything. They'd gotten to be friends of sorts these last few weeks—Adam spent a lot of his free time at the bar, as did Lex—and Greg probably knew he'd never seen this girl before in his life.

Grabbing the bottle, she chugged down half of it before glancing up at him. "Thank you," she mouthed.

Even as he cursed himself for getting involved in human problems, he left his arm around her shoulders, effectively body-blocking the human male who was still lurking behind them. But Adam knew he was still there because he could feel his eyes burning into the back of his head.

"Who the fuck is this, Faye?"

The accusation, shouted right behind her, nearly made her choke on her beer. Putting on a show, because maybe he liked to stir the pot a bit himself, Adam rubbed her back as she set the bottle on the bar and grabbed the napkins he handed her. Why couldn't the guy just take the hint and find someone else to harass? Adam really didn't want to get blood on his Ralph Lauren cardigan sweater. Glancing down at it, he sighed. He knew he should've worn the dark blue one and not the cream and tan.

Since the lady's pursuer obviously wasn't willing to be ignored, Adam turned to face him. The guy's dark eyes were lit with a rage that didn't seem appropriate for the situation. Or, hell, maybe it was. Maybe he was her ex and didn't appreciate some new guy treading on his property. It didn't really matter. She didn't want his company. And he needed to take the hint. Adam didn't smile, but he did hold out his hand. "Hey. I'm Adam, Faye's boyfriend."

The douche didn't even look at his offer of a civilized meeting. "Faye doesn't have a *boyfriend*." He practically spit the word in Adam's face.

Adam dropped his hand, cocked his head, and gave him a puzzled expression. "That's funny you say that. Because I'm sitting right fucking here beside her."

The woman—Faye—finally turned around. "Jeff, this is Adam. My b-boyfriend." Her stutter was barely noticeable. "Adam, this is Jeff. An old *friend* from school."

Tearing his eyes from Adam, Jeff stared at her for a hard minute. He clearly didn't believe her. Adam was about resigned to the fact that he was, in fact, going to get blood all over his sweater when Jeff told her, "We'll talk later." Then he turned on his heel and walked back to the table where he'd left his drink, shouldering through the people on the dance floor who didn't see him coming in time to get out of his way.

Faye watched him go, then turned to face the bar again, her hands on her cheeks for a moment before she finished off her beer. "I knew I shouldn't have come tonight," she said quietly as she climbed up on the empty stool beside her.

"So why did you?" Adam asked as he joined her back at the bar, shutting out the crowd behind them.

She stilled, turning her head to look at him with little frown wrinkles between her eyebrows. "Excuse me?"

"Why'd you come if you knew that asshole was just going to harass you? Who is he?" Normally, he wouldn't get into her business like that. But being that he'd put himself between this douchebag and the woman he obviously was willing to bully into being with him, Adam thought he should probably know what he'd just gotten himself into. "Is he your ex or something?"

She shook her head, still frowning at him. "No."

"He seems to think he has some kind of claim on you." Adam's wolf prowled beneath his ribcage at the thought. He didn't like hearing that any more than Adam liked saying it. He forced him down. This woman wasn't either of their concern.

She silently studied his face for a minute longer, then she slid off her stool and got her coat, folding it over her arm before she picked up her purse. "Thanks for the beer." She paused. "And the interference. But I can take it from here."

Adam grabbed her arm as she started to walk away. "Where are you going?"

"Look," she told him. "I can take a hint. You obviously don't want any company." She tried to soften her words with a smile. "And I don't want to intrude on whatever you've got going on here, so thanks again for helping me. But you're right. I'm just gonna go home."

He still didn't let go of her arm. "What about your admirer?"

She glanced over in the direction he went. "Looks like Lucy has him distracted for the moment, so I'm just gonna sneak out."

Adam had no idea if what she said was true or not because he couldn't take his eyes off her face. "Stay," he found himself saying. "Don't let him chase you off."

"He's not." She looked at Adam pointedly.

Ah. So it was him. He was the asshole now. He let go of her arm. "Okay, don't let *me* chase you off. Stay. Enjoy the party."

She glanced in the direction of the front door again and, this time, he followed her gaze. Her admirer had noticed their conversation and was now blocking her path to the door, his eyes glued to Faye.

"Come on," Adam told her. "Stay. I promise I'll be nice." Well, as much as he could be after being dragged there against his will by his well-meaning friends.

"I didn't lead him on or anything, you know," she said. "I'm just nice to him when he comes in to get a coffee. Like I am to all of the customers. Or when a group of us hangs out. Jeff just thinks it's more than it is, and once he gets his mind set on something, it's hard to shake him off."

"Okay," Adam told her.

She hesitated, but after another quick glance toward the front door and the man waiting for her, she hung her coat back over the stool and set her purse back on the bar. He waited until she was back up on her seat, and then flagged Greg down for two more beers.

"Bud Light?" Adam asked her when she picked up her bottle. "Really?"

"Babydoll?" she countered.

He shrugged. "It was all I could come up with at the time."

Adam took in her delicate features as she smiled and waved at another girl on the other side of the bar, her knee bouncing up and down with the music. Seemed her natural good humor had been restored. And it *was* natural. He could practically feel the positive vibrations emanating from her.

"So, you work at the coffee shop?"

She set down her beer and nodded. "Yeah, at The Java House." She eyed his face and shoulders. "I don't think I've ever seen you there."

"I don't drink coffee."

"We've got other stuff there, too. Tea. Smoothies. Sandwiches."

"How long have you worked there?"

He could see her adding the time up in her head. "About eight years. Ever since I got out of high school."

That made her about twenty-six. She looked younger. "You never wanted to do anything else?"

Those little wrinkles appeared again, and then she nodded as if everything just suddenly clicked. "So, you're one of *those* guys."

"What guys?"

Her eyes traveled over his clean-shaven face and neck, down to his designer cardigan sweater. "The kind that think they're too good to date a girl who works at a coffee shop. Even if it is a fake relationship."

His thumb rubbed the label of his expensive beer, still full. "I think you took my question the wrong way," he started, knowing damn well she hadn't.

"No," she said. "I didn't. But it's okay. You can't help who you are."

It was said in such an accepting manner that there was no way he should take offense to what she'd said. And yet, somehow, he did. "What the hell is that supposed to mean?"

She'd just opened her mouth to answer, when they were suddenly overwhelmed by the scent of cheap, flowery perfume.

"Hey, Faye!"

It was only because he was watching her so closely that he noticed the way she braced herself before she turned to smile at the woman she'd waved at earlier. Jumping off her stool, Faye accidentally elbowed him in the stomach as she reached up to hug the taller woman. "Sorry," she mumbled to him as she wrapped her arms around her friend and gave her a warm hug.

Watching her, he tried to imagine what it felt like to be wrapped up in all of that warmth and sunshine, and he was suddenly jealous.

"Margo," Faye said over the music when they were done. "This is Adam. Adam, this is my friend, Margo."

He shook off the unfamiliar feeling. Margo's brown eyes shone with devilish delight as she eyed him up and down. "Nice to meet you."

Adam nodded at her, but didn't return her enthusiasm. "You, too."

With the smile still on her face and without taking her eyes from him, she said to Faye, "He's a grumbly one, isn't he?"

Faye's laughing blue eyes met Adam's. "He's not so bad."

Margo didn't look so sure. "I'll take your word for it." Abruptly, she turned her attention to Faye. "You're still coming to the movies with us next weekend, right?"

"Oh...uh...sure," Faye told her.

Margo's sharp brown eyes shot back over to him. "Bring Adam."

Immediately, he threw up his hands. "Oh, no. Sorry, I can't."

She cocked her head and gave him a way too innocent look. "You're going to let your girlfriend go by herself?"

Faye stared at him with pleading blue eyes that tugged at something in his chest.

Goddamnit.

FAYE

Faye held her breath—which was hard for her, because this guy smelled really, really good—as the good-looking stranger she'd just dumped all of her problems on tried to think of a good excuse to back out of their brand spanking new pretend relationship before it even had a chance to start.

But to her surprise, he let out a sigh and told Margo, "Maybe I can change my plans."

His answer was far from promising that he'd actually carry through with going, but if it would get Margo off her back, even temporarily, she'd take it.

Margo's eyebrows rose in surprise. "Good. Great!" She clasped her hands together in front of her chest. "I'm gonna go drag one of these unsuspecting guys onto the dance floor. I'll see you both Saturday, then!" She pointed at Faye. "I'll call you later."

Oh, I bet you will. Faye grinned until her cheeks hurt as Margo smiled at the two of them in turn and finally left. As soon as she was gone, Faye turned her back to the crowd and picked up her beer, chugging down nearly half of it before setting it back down on the bar.

"Is your friend always so presumptuous?"

"She only did that because she doesn't believe you and I are actually dating."

"We're not."

"I know that. And you know that. But please don't tell anyone else that. I'll never get Jeff off my back if he finds out the truth." She was only half joking when she said it but, honestly, maybe that wasn't a bad idea...

"Look," her new fake boyfriend said, and she barely held back a moan. She knew what was coming.

Before he could say anything, or go back on his promise to be her date for the movie, she started talking. "Margo isn't really a friend. I mean, she is. But she's not. She's a frenemy."

One eyebrow went up. "A what?"

"I've known her most of my life," she went on. "Actually, I've known almost everyone here that long. Except for you."

"I still don't understand."

How to explain... "Margo and I are friends only because we've known each other forever. But..." She struggled to find the words. Only someone from a small town would know that it caused a lot less drama on the group of friends overall to just pretend to like everyone. "She's not really a good person. She's also not a bad person. She's just always had this...thing...that she needs to be involved in everyone else's business. Of course, that's because this is such a small town. It's kind of hard to avoid being in everyone's business." She was babbling now, but she couldn't stop herself. "So, what I'm saying is that she's not exactly a mean person, she just gets way too excited over everyone else's life. Especially mine, for some reason. And Jeff, the guy who's been trying to get me to go out with him, is her cousin, and so Margo is always trying to think of ways to force us together, hoping that I'll give in and—"

"Wait," he cut her off. "Do you want something to happen with him?"

"What?" Faye was taken aback by the sharpness of his tone. "No."

"Why not?"

"Why not?" she repeated stupidly. "Because I'm not attracted to him. And he kind of..." She trailed off. Something about the way Adam's entire body was leaning toward her as he waited for her answer made her cautious of saying anything more. Jeff had a thick skull and had a hard time taking no for an answer, but that didn't mean she wanted to cause him any trouble. And her instincts were telling her that her new boyfriend, fake or not, would cause a *lot* of it.

"He what?" he repeated.

Faye shook her head. "Nothing." She wasn't about to admit that Jeff scared her a little sometimes.

"Faye."

Her eyes were drawn back to his, almost against her will. His were bright green, almost abnormally so. She blinked.

"Tell me."

The words were spoken so softly, she didn't know how she even heard them. Yet, she did. And she had no choice but to answer him. Before she realized what she was doing, her mouth opened and the words came out almost against her will. "He scares me a little sometimes." Immediately, she tried to backtrack. She *really* didn't want to cause him any trouble. The town would never let her forget it. "He's just so big and...and..." She frowned. Jeff was about the same size as Adam. But Adam, even with his grumpy exterior, didn't frighten her the way Jeff did. Not even when he was knocking back beers, like he was doing now. Quite the contrary. She felt perfectly safe.

"Has he done something to scare you?"

She blinked as she tried to think. "No. Not really. I'm probably just being silly."

He leaned back, and she gratefully sucked in a lungful of air. "If your instincts are telling you to be cautious of this guy, I'd listen to them."

"Okay." She didn't know what else to say. She was still trying to get more oxygen into her lungs. "Are you really going to come to the movies with me?" she asked when she could breathe normally again.

His eyes roamed over her face, and he surprised her by saying, "Yeah. I'll come with you. If you want me to."

"That would be great." She smiled as relief flooded her system. To be honest, she'd been trying to think of a way to get out of it just so she wouldn't have to go alone and have Jeff up her butt all night. But it was her best friend's birthday. And she couldn't leave Jules alone with the wolves, so to speak. And she couldn't ask her not to invite Jeff and Margo. It would cause way too much drama in their little group, and the town, for that matter. When you lived in a place with a population of less than eight hundred people, and had since you were born, it wasn't easy to avoid things without becoming the town pariah. You couldn't just make something up, because everyone knew what you were doing at any given moment, including what you ate for dinner and how often you peed.

At least, that's what it felt like, sometimes.

But still, Faye wouldn't trade the life she had in Fairplay for anyone else's. There were good things about living in a small town. Despite the gossip and the lack of decent jobs, people cared about each other, and they were there for each other when it really mattered. And Faye always chose to focus on the positive.

And on that note...

She slid off her stool and grabbed Adam by the wrist. "Come on."

He tilted his head and gave her a look of curiosity, but didn't budge off his stool. "Where are we going?"

"It's New Year's. Let's dance." She gave his arm another little tug.

But he shook his head. "I don't dance."

Her smile faltered, but just a bit before she kicked it up another notch. A two-step was going on, and she loved to two-step. "Aww, come on. It's not hard. I can teach you."

Adam eyed her. "I didn't say I *couldn't* dance. I said I don't. And I'm not going to, no matter how much you smile at me like that."

His eyes dropped to her mouth as the smile she'd tried so hard to keep in place slipped again. She tried to keep the disappointment from her face as she let go of his wrist. "Oh. Okay." Not knowing what else to say, she grabbed her bottle of beer and leaned back against the bar to watch the other couples as they passed by. Tears threatened at his brusque dismissal, but Faye blinked them away. She wasn't usually so sensitive, but she'd had a hell of a day and all she'd wanted to do was come celebrate the new year with friends. And dance. And if her new fake boyfriend didn't want to help her out on that front, well, it's not like they were exclusive or anything. She would just go find someone else to dance with. Most of the guys who'd grown up in this town had figured out real quick that they'd better learn how if they wanted a chance with any of the girls they liked. But she also knew that as soon as she left Adam's side, Jeff would be on her like a bur.

An awkward silence grew between them as all of this ran through her head. Faye looked around, desperate to find someone she liked to talk to. But everyone was either already dancing or engaged with other people. Chewing on the corner of her bottom lip, she fought the disappointment that threatened to rise within her.

"Come dance with me, Faye!"

Her head snapped up to find Alan George—football quarterback and homecoming king in high school—beckoning her onto the floor from the other side of a crowded table. He still dated his homecoming queen, Angela, but Faye had already seen her dancing with one of her brothers.

Knowing that Angela wouldn't mind, Faye grinned and nodded, then turned to set her beer down on the bar.

Green eyes caught hers. "Where the hell are you going?"

"To dance," she told him. Turns out Margo was right. He *was* grumpy.

He didn't say anything else, but she didn't give him much of a chance as she walked away, dodging the other couples and meeting Alan in the middle of the dance floor. Tall, lean, and blond, he let out a "Let's go, girl!" and spun her around once before clasping one of her hands with his and settling the other on her hip.

Faye laughed and eased effortlessly into the dance. Even though Alan was quite a bit taller than she was, they'd danced together many times since high school and moved together almost as well as him and Angela. Halfway around the floor, they caught up with his girlfriend, and he leaned out and kissed her on the cheek as they passed by. Angela waved at Faye and laughed as Alan spun her around again.

By the time the song ended, Faye was out of breath.

"Again?" Alan asked her as Garth Brooks came over the speakers.

She nodded happily and laughed as he threw her into a spin as Garth sang about not going down till the sun came up.

Adam could sit over there and brood all he wanted to. Faye was going to enjoy herself and ring in the new year in style. And if the mere presence of her new fake boyfriend watching her from the bar kept Jeff away from her, she would be forever grateful.

Hell, she might even give him a kiss at midnight.

ADAM

For a damsel in distress, Faye was having a mighty fine damn time.

Without *him*, he might add.

The male who'd saved her.

Adam scowled as she danced past, completely ignoring him as she grinned up at her dance partner, a guy who looked like he was still in high school and who he'd seen snuggling up with another woman not thirty minutes before.

"Your scowl is extra scowly right now." Lex Chapman, the only wolf Adam fully trusted with his life and who scared the actual hell out of him at the same time, took a seat on the empty stool that Faye had abandoned, despite the fact her coat was still slung across the back. With his shaved head and neck tattoos, he was the exact opposite of Adam in the way he looked and dressed. Biker boots, torn jeans and old T-shirts were Lex's go to, and the two of them always got strange looks when people saw them hanging out together.

Lex waved down Greg and ordered a dark beer.

"I don't know how you drink that stuff," Adam told him.

Lex picked up the mug of Guinness Greg set down in front of him and tilted it toward the bottle in Adam's hand. "I don't know how you drink those girly beers."

"An IPA isn't girly."

"If you say so." Lex toasted him with a smirk and took a big swallow of his beer.

Adam went back to keeping an eye on Faye. He told himself that the only reason he kept his eyes glued to her was to make sure her not-so-secret admirer didn't give her any more problems, but the way his wolf was prowling beneath his skin begged to differ.

He felt Lex's dark eyes on him for only a few seconds before he saw him look over his shoulder and find the object of Adam's undivided attention. "Who's the hottie?"

"Faye," Adam answered automatically. "My new fake girlfriend."

"It doesn't look so fake to me," Lex observed.

Adam turned his body toward his friend, but he couldn't manage to pull his eyes from the ball of energy and sunshine lighting up the dance floor. He could practically see a glow of warmth around her, drawing people to her. "I just met her tonight. Some guy was harassing her, so I pretended to be her boyfriend so he'd leave her the hell alone."

"If you're her boyfriend, why aren't you out there dancing with her?"

Because he had to be a rude, stubborn ass when she'd asked him. A decision he was regretting more and more.

Adam's upper lip lifted in a snarl as he watched her partner's big hand slide "innocently" over the generous curve of her ass.

That was it. He'd had enough. Adam slammed his empty beer bottle down on the bar. "I'll be back," he told Lex.

"Go get her, tiger," he said, his eyes glued to the television screen behind the bar as he watched the New Year's celebration happening in Times Square.

The whole time Adam was weaving his way through the dancers, he wondered what the hell he was doing. He still didn't have a good answer by the time he reached her, but he was going to do it anyway.

When Faye's partner noticed him blocking their way, he pulled her to a stop. "You know this guy?" he asked her, lifting his chin toward Adam.

She looked back over her shoulder. "Hey!" she greeted Adam. The smile she gave him nearly blinded him. "This is my friend, Adam," she told her dance partner.

"I'm cutting in," he informed her. Then his eyes flicked over to the guy she was dancing with. He was tall, but he was skinny. If it came down to a fight, Adam would easily win, even if he didn't have the strength of a shifter.

But the guy just grinned amiably and handed Faye over to Adam. "Here you go, man. She's all yours. Have fun!"

Adam took Faye into the circle of his arms as he scowled after him. But his attention was quickly diverted by the feel of all the womanly softness he now held tight against him.

"I thought you didn't dance," she said as his eyes met the twinkle of amusement in hers.

Loosening his hold just enough to let her breathe, he frowned. "I changed my mind."

Adam didn't like the way her mouth twitched as she fought to keep the amusement off her face. "Okay," was all she said. "We should probably start doing it then before we get run over."

Right then, the music changed and something slow and angsty came over the speakers. He didn't recognize the song, but it didn't matter. His mother loved to dance, and she'd made damn sure Adam could hold his own on a dance floor, whether it was a ballroom or a country bar or anywhere in between. Not that he'd wanted to learn, but there were times—such as this one—when he was mighty glad she'd been so insistent.

Pulling their joined hands close to his chest, he tightened his other arm around her until he could feel the fullness of her breasts pressed against him and started shuffling his feet. As they started to move together, their hips would touch off and on, and much as he tried to fight it, Adam's cock thickened painfully in his designer jeans. He dug his fingers into the silky material of her shirt, gathering it into his fist as he tried to get himself under control. He couldn't recall what color the shirt was, or anything else she was wearing, for that matter. He was too immersed in the way she felt. The way she smelled. Like she was already under his skin, dancing with his wolf.

Faye was a bit stiff in his arms at first, but gradually, she relaxed. She even tucked her head under his chin, fitting against him like she fucking belonged there, her scent in his nose and her body moving perfectly with his as he led them slowly around the dance floor. Just like she would in bed.

He didn't know how he knew that.

He just did.

They hadn't made even one full circle around the room before the hair on the back of his neck rose and tingles ran up and down his spine. Adam met the eyes of her spurned admirer. He was glaring daggers at them, his posture stiff and angry. But pissing him off was only part of the reason Adam insisted on holding her so up close and personal. The other reasons were...well, he didn't fucking know. All he knew was that she felt damn fucking good.

"So, Adam," Faye raised her head and looked up at him. She was even prettier this close up. There were no thick layers of makeup or weird colors on her face, just fresh skin and long eyelashes and glossy lips that he would bet his life savings were naturally that color.

He was quickly becoming obsessed with those lips.

"What brings you to our cozy little town?" She raised her eyebrows in question as she waited for his answer.

"What makes you think I'm new here?"

She gave him a look, and then glanced around the bar before coming back to him. "Because just about everyone who lives in this town can fit into this bar, and I've lived here my whole life. So, trust me, if someone who looked like you had come along sooner, I would've heard about it."

"What's wrong with the way I look?"

Her clear blue eyes darkened as they traveled over his face and shoulders, or maybe it was just a trick of the light. "Not a damn thing," she said. "As a matter of fact—and I say this at the risk of making your head swell—you and your friend over there at the bar make the rest of the guys in this town look like backwoods swine."

A ripple of possession ran through him at her including Lex in that statement, and his arms tightened around her as he navigated them in a turn around another couple and forced her eyes back on him. "I wouldn't call them 'swine.' Pigs are actually really clean if you take them out of the mud."

Faye threw her head back and laughed. He wasn't sure what was so funny, exactly, but he wasn't about to say or do anything that would wipe that expression of joy from her face.

The song ended, and "Touch" by July Talk started playing.

As the majority of people on the dance floor headed for the bar, Faye tried to pull away from him, but Adam pulled her back and looped her arms around his neck as he swayed back and forth to the intro. When the beat picked up, he took her hand again and moved her into a faster step, spinning her around just to hear the sweet sound of her laughter.

The deep gravel baritone of the male singer rumbled through his blood, the lyrics about letting a woman in hitting Adam in a certain kind of way.

He, too, wanted to slice open his skin and pull her inside. It was the only way he'd ever feel close enough to her. He wanted to feel her blood race with his. Hear her heartbeat in his ears...

The song ended way too soon. Faye was breathing hard, her chest rising and falling deliciously against his own. Adam inhaled, breathing her into his lungs, allowing the scent of her to absorb into his cells. She stared up at him for a long time, and Adam didn't need her to tell him what she was feeling in that moment, because he was feeling the same thing.

Another song came on, breaking the spell.

"You never answered my question," she said as he led her over to Lex and the two cold beers waiting for them.

Adam handed hers to her and took a long drink of his before asking, "What question is that?"

"What brought you two here," she reminded him, glancing at Lex with a smile.

"Lex, this is Faye. Faye, Lex."

Lex gave her a nod. "Nice to meet you, Faye."

"You, too," she told him.

"Work," Adam told her.

"Work?"

"Yeah," he said. "We're here for work. Specifically, to help out our friend Riko with some things."

"Oh, I know Riko. He grew up here, but he moved away right after high school. He was a few years ahead of me, but my brother graduated with him. He comes into the coffee shop sometimes with Addison." She gave him a quizzical look. "Does that mean you aren't staying?"

"I hadn't planned on it, no," he told her honestly.

Her face fell just a bit, but she hid it so fast, he almost wondered if he'd imagined it. Still, his wolf growled at the thought of her being unhappy. "That's too bad," she said softly, her eyes on his.

"Faye! Come dance with us!"

She smiled and waved at the group of girls on the dance floor, but hesitated to join them. Adam tore his eyes away from her and took another drink. He needed to get his shit together. He wasn't here to make eyes at a pretty girl. "Go on," he told her. "Go dance."

She glanced nervously in the direction of a rowdy corner of the bar where Jeff was leading the toasts. Adam hadn't missed the way he'd been keeping one eye on Faye the entire night. "You don't have to worry about him," he told her. "Me and Lex here will cut him off if he tries anything tonight. Right, Lex?"

"Sure," he said as he waved Greg down for another beer. "I'm always up for a fight."

"No," Faye told him. "No fighting." Then she backed off a bit. "Although I appreciate the gesture. But I can handle Jeff."

Adam caught her eyes with his. "I know you can, but you don't have to. Not tonight, at least."

She gave him a smile that made his chest hurt. "Thank you. You're the best fake boyfriend ever." And with that, she leaned over and kissed him on the cheek near the corner of his mouth.

Adam turned his head on instinct, but she was gone before he could capture her lips with his, hurrying out onto the dance floor to join her girlfriends. His wolf pushed at his ribcage, eager to taste her. Gritting his teeth and wondering what the fuck was wrong with him, Adam forced himself to let her go.

When he turned back to the bar, Lex was staring at him. "What?" he growled.

"Nothin'," his friend told him with a smirk. "Not a goddamn thing."

CHAPTER 4

FAYE

The bell over the door jingled, and Faye groaned as she hauled herself to her feet and fixed her apron. The morning rush had just ended, and she'd already burned her fingers with the milk steamer when she'd tried to wipe it down with her bare hand instead of the wet cloth she was supposed to use.

It was her own fault, though. Her mind just wasn't on what she was doing. Instead, it was stuck on replay of everything that happened at the New Year's party two nights ago. Specifically, the way it had felt to be wrapped up in the strong arms of her new fake boyfriend. Her new fake boyfriend who was coming with her to the movies on Saturday.

She was still wearing a dreamy smile when she came out of the back to greet her next customer. But it froze on her face when she saw who'd come in. Faye stopped and blinked, but quickly got it together and approached the counter, her smile—if a bit forced—back in place. "Hey, Jeff. What can I get for you?"

Resting his crossed arms on the counter, he looked up at her. "You can tell me who that asshole is you were with the other night."

"Do you want a coffee with that? Or are you just here to interrogate me?"

He narrowed his eyes a little at her snappy tone, but for the love of god, she was really tired of defending herself with this guy. Why the hell couldn't he take a hint? Instead, he had to come in here and ruin a perfectly good morning—burns and all—with his overly possessive attitude. They'd never even gone on a date, for Christ's sake.

"Tell me who he is, Faye."

Crossing her arms in front of her chest, she quickly dropped them again when his eyes went right to her boobs. "I introduced you at Greg's. There's nothing else to know."

"Yeah, see. Somehow, I don't believe you."

She looked desperately toward the door, praying someone else would come in and save her from this conversation. "What's not to believe, Jeff? That I could possibly have a boyfriend?"

He made a disbelieving noise. "Come on, Faye. You know I don't think anything like that. Just that you suddenly have one that no one else knew about. Not even Margo."

She had to admit he had a point there. As the town's unofficial and unneeded keeper, Margo made it her business to know everyone else's since she was around ten years old. "Like I said the other night, it's kind of a new thing," Faye told him. "I haven't really had a lot of time to introduce him to anyone before the New Year's party."

"So where's he from?"

Shit. Frantically, she thought back to the few things she and Adam talked about at the bar. Hadn't he said something about coming out to help Riko with something? Which meant he knew Riko from Oklahoma. "Oklahoma," she told him. "He's a friend of Riko Silvano's."

"Don't know why that motherfucker moved back here."

Faye couldn't tell if he was really wondering or if he held some kind of grudge against Riko. "I think he did it for Addison."

"Yeah, maybe." His tone said he didn't really give a shit why Riko came home, but his gaze was hard. "Seems like his friend moved in awful fast." *On my property.* He didn't say the words out loud, but the meaning was clear in the way he crowded her, even with the counter between them, and the way his eyes roved over her face and body.

Faye resisted the urge to drop down behind the counter and cover her burning cheeks with her hands. Anger, hot and unfamiliar, rose up inside of her. It wasn't a feeling that Faye was used to. She was a person who could always see the positive side of things and never let anything get her down for long. But there was nothing good about the way Jeff was looking at her right then. Something in his eyes was making her extremely uneasy. Something she'd never noticed before. And it went way beyond just an annoying crush.

The words bubbled up and came out of her mouth before she had a chance to think about what she was saying. Maybe it was the only line of defense she could think of. Maybe it was her earlier daydreaming getting out of control. Or maybe it was just pure desperation. "Actually, Adam and I are engaged."

She'd finally managed to make him speechless. At least for a few seconds. "Get the fuck out."

Faye forced a bright smile. "It's true. He proposed on New Year's." Not *exactly* true. He'd accepted her kiss at midnight with his jaw clenched and his eyes open, and then walked her out to her car shortly after when Jeff's staring had worn on her to the point that she'd just wanted to go home.

He pushed his weight off the counter and straightened to his full height. "Then where's the ring?"

She smiled even brighter. "We're gonna go pick it out together."

Jeff gave her a look. "A man proposes to a girl and doesn't even know her taste enough to have a ring picked out for her?"

"Or maybe he just has enough consideration for her to let her pick out something she'll really like. After all, she'll be wearing it forever."

"Maybe not forever," he told her. With a tight smile, he took a few steps back. "I'm gonna skip that coffee today. But I'll see you Saturday."

"Yeah. We'll be there." She gave him a little wave as he walked out the door. Then she started cleaning the espresso machine like she didn't have a care in the world, even though she'd already cleaned it, just in case he was standing outside somewhere watching her. Faye was grateful when one of the local cops came in to distract her, though she would've been happier if he'd pulled up just a little bit sooner.

While she was serving Ted his free coffee, a few more people wandered in, and soon the coffee shop was filled with the lunch crowd. Faye had no time to worry about Jeff for the rest of the day, and she'd almost forgotten about his strange visit until she was practically assaulted by Jules when her shift was over.

"You're ENGAGED?? And you didn't tell me??"

Faye shushed her as she pulled her coat on and hustled them both outside before everyone in the coffee shop heard. "No."

Her best friend of twenty years stopped walking and blocked her path, forcing Faye to stop too. "But Margo told me that Jeff told her that you told *him* you were engaged to the hot new guy I didn't get to meet on New Year's because I was sick."

Faye rolled her eyes. "That part is true."

Jules frowned, confused. "Which part?"

"All of that," she told her. "I did tell him that. But only to get him off my back." Grabbing her friend's arm, she started walking toward her car parked just down the street. It was only late afternoon and already the temperature was dropping, and she wanted to get to the museum and get through a box or two before it got colder. Faye worked at the South Park City Museum—a recreation of the historic 1880s gold rush town Fairplay had grown from—when it was open during the summer. In the middle of winter, like it was now, it more resembled the ghost town it actually was, and she didn't like to be there by herself after the sun went down. Besides the fact that there was no heat in the buildings, it was just downright creepy being there alone with the ghosts of the past.

"I don't understand," Jules told her. "So, you're not engaged?"

"No."

"Okay, well, that's going to be a problem because Margo is, at this very moment, running around town, telling everyone the good news."

Faye shot her friend a worried glance. "I had to do it. Jeff is getting seriously creepy with me."

Jules stopped again. "What has he done?"

Faye sighed, glancing up and down Main Street to make sure no one else was within hearing distance. Then she threw her hands up with a shrug. "Nothing, really. At least nothing that I can point a finger at. But he came into the shop today and was giving me the third degree about Adam."

"The fake fiancé."

"Fake boyfriend, at the time," Faye clarified. "But nothing I said was making Jeff back off, so I blurted out that we were engaged."

"Did it work?"

Faye shrugged again. "It threw him off and he left."

Jules pulled her coat closed as a gust of wind kicked up around them. "You know this is all gonna blow up in your face as soon as the rumor gets to Adam and he shuts it down."

She did know that. Unless... "Unless I can talk him into going along with it. At least temporarily. Just until Jeff finds someone else to obsess over."

"Good luck with that. He's had the hots for you since we were in eighth grade. He's just never had the guts to pursue you until now."

Faye chewed on her thumbnail as she desperately tried to think of another way to get Jeff off her back, but she honestly couldn't think of anything else that would. "The only problem is, I have no idea where to even find Adam to talk him into doing it."

Jules grinned. "I know exactly where to find him."

Faye's eyes snapped up to her friend's face. "You do? Where?"

"He works at the garage with his scary looking friend. I just took my car in to get an oil change."

"That's great!" Faye continued walking toward her car with Jules right beside her, her stomach twisting up at the thought that Adam worked just down the road from where she lived. "Maybe I can get there before Margo thinks of doing the same thing so she can get details from him."

"Except..."

Faye stopped. She didn't like that tone. "Except what?"

She grabbed Faye's hand. "Except I might have already said something to one of the other guys at the shop."

"Who?"

"That other new guy. The scary one with the hot neck tattoo. Lex."

"Jesus, Jules! Why the hell would you do that?"

"Because I got the text from Margo when he was ringing me up. You know how she likes to run to me with news about you. It's like we're still in high school and she's trying to prove to me that she's better friends with you or something." She rolled her eyes. "Anyway, I was so shocked I read it out loud and he was right there." She gave Faye an apologetic look. "I'm sorry. If I'd known what was going on, I wouldn't have done that." There was no accusation in her tone. No hurt feelings. But Faye still felt the need to explain.

"I'm sorry, too. I should've told you right away. I wasn't trying to keep it from you or anything; I just knew I was gonna see you today and I could tell you in person."

But Jules waved away her apology. "Don't worry about it. I just wish I'd kept my damn mouth shut for once." They stared at each other for a moment until Jules said, "So, what are you gonna do now?"

"I guess I need to go see Adam and try to explain."

Jules nodded. "Probably a good idea."

"Yeah."

"Yeah."

"Am I being stupid?" Faye blurted out.

"For talking to Adam?"

"No. For making up this entire story instead of just telling Jeff to fuck off."

"Yes," Jules told her without hesitation. "Except..."

Faye held her breath. "Except *what*?"

"Except I know Jeff as well as you do. And he's as stubborn as those damn cows that Addison lets roam around town and won't let anyone eat. I think if you told him to fuck off, he'd just take it as more of a challenge."

Faye's heart sank. Jules was right. "Okay, then. My only other option is to talk Adam into going along with this stupid plan until Jeff loses interest or I die. Whichever comes first."

"Right."

"Right," Faye repeated. She gave her friend a hug. "I'll let you know how it goes. Do you need a ride anywhere?"

Jules shook her head. "No. I'm good. Call me later."

Faye nodded and got into her car. She glanced in her side mirror to make sure there weren't any cars coming and saw Jeff pull up in front of the coffee shop in his oversized truck.

She gave Jules a wave and pulled away from the curb, grateful that her friend was there to keep him from following her. Still, the hair rose on the back of her neck, and she knew he was watching her drive away. Faye took the first turn she could, only releasing the breath she was holding when she didn't see him behind her.

CHAPTER 5

ADAM

$\mathcal{A}$dam sensed her before he saw her. This wasn't entirely unusual. His heightened sense of sight, smell, and hearing meant he knew when someone was there before most people did.

But this was different. This was an awareness he'd never felt before. Something that made his wolf whine inside of him and scratch at his ribs to escape.

Faye.

He knew right away that she was nervous, a little scared even, and he wanted to drop the torque wrench into the old Chevy he was working on and rush into the lobby, find out what was going on, and then kill whoever it was that was making her feel this way.

But he did none of those things. Instead, he kept on working like any normal male would. Doing anything else would expose him as something "other." And although he worked there at the garage with the majority of the local wolf pack, there were also a half dozen or so non-shifter males and females who worked there with him.

Rocky, Adam's best friend and companion for the past four and a half years, give or take a month or two, lifted his furry white head and stared at the door to the lobby. His long tail thumped on the concrete floor as though he, too, sensed an old friend he hadn't seen in a long time. Adam watched him with curiosity. Rocky was half wolf, and although he was well trained and pretty chill, he didn't normally take to strangers right off. Sometimes it took him months to warm up to a new person.

A few seconds later, Tommy opened the door and yelled over the sound of the machines and Judas Priest blaring from the radio in the back. "Adam! You've got a lady requesting you!"

Acting surprised, he set down his wrench on the bench behind him and picked up a rag to wipe his hands. "Rocky." Adam made a sign with his hand and Rocky hefted his large frame up onto his giant paws and padded after him. He would've been fine left where he was, but Adam was curious to see how he would interact with Faye after the interest he'd shown when she walked into the shop. Dropping the rag on a table, he pulled open the door that led to the office and motioned Rocky through, then followed him.

Faye stood in the far corner of the waiting room with her back to him, watching the snow flurries out the window. Her pretty hair fell in loose waves just past her shoulders. Her coat was folded over her arm, and she was wearing a long-sleeved emerald-green shirt and black pants that hugged the curves of her ass and thighs. A pair of worn sneakers covered her feet. The heater kicked on and her scent—like a warm summer field basking in the sunshine —washed over him, warming him from the inside out and making him hard all at the same time.

Rocky stepped in front of him with his nose in the air, honed in on Faye, and headed toward her.

Worried the huge mutt would scare her, Adam said quietly, "Rocky. Hold."

He immediately stopped and sat, but let out a whimper, his blue eyes glued to the woman who'd just turned around to face them. A huge smile broke out on her face the moment she saw the wolf dog. "Hey there, gorgeous," she told him softly.

The whimper turned into a full-blown whine.

"You're gonna give him a bigger head than he already has talking to him like that," Adam said with a hint of amusement.

Her eyes flew to his face, then back to the wolf dog.

"Don't worry about him," Adam tried to reassure her. "Unless my life is in danger, he won't move until I tell him to."

"Oh, it's okay," she said. "He can come and say hello."

"Are you sure?"

"Yeah," she told him, still smiling. "Absolutely."

Adam hesitated for a moment, and then gave Rocky the command to move freely about the room. "At ease, Rocky."

Immediately, he stood and closed the distance between himself and Faye. She held still as he gave her a good sniff, then his large head ducked under her hand so she could pet him. Faye laughed and did as he asked. Adam didn't worry that he would hurt her. The only people that got on Rocky's shit list were assholes. And Faye wasn't an asshole. He was just so large and reserved that he tended to scare people who didn't know him. But it didn't look like he had anything to worry about with Faye. "Looks like he likes you."

"What's his name?"

"Rocky."

"That's a good name for such a sweet boy," she cooed.

Adam raised an eyebrow, but his ferocious guard dog practically arched like a cat under the touch of her hands as she rubbed them over his head and down his back. He was so big next to her—his back nearly hit her waist—she didn't even need to lean over. All Adam could do was shake his head and change the subject. "So, I hear that we're engaged now." He assumed that's why she was there.

Her smile froze, then fell from her face as she straightened, her fingers curling into Rocky's white and gray fur, and gave Adam an apologetic look. "I'm so sorry, Adam. That's what I came here to talk to you about." She glanced over at Lex behind the counter, ringing out a customer. "Do you have a minute?"

Rocky stared at him, waiting patiently for his answer so he could get back to his petting. "If you give me about ten minutes, I'll be done for the day. We can grab dinner and talk."

Her shoulders relaxed, and she gave him a grateful look. "That would be great. I just need to stop by the museum first, if that's okay?"

Adam racked his brain, trying to remember seeing a building in this town that could possibly house priceless artwork and came up blank. "Museum?"

"Yeah, I work there in the summer when it's open. I just need to grab some boxes to take home."

He still had no idea where the museum was, but he nodded. "Sure. Give me a few minutes to finish up."

"Can Rocky stay with me?" she asked.

"I don't think I'd be able to convince him to leave," he told her honestly. "I'll be right back. There's water and coffee over there if you want some." He pointed to the other side of the waiting room.

"I'm good, thanks," she told him, taking a seat in the chair behind her. Rocky followed her, sitting beside her and laying his head on her lap.

Adam shook his head at the picture they made, and went back into the garage to finish putting the Chevy back together for his customer so it would be all ready to pick up in the morning. Then he went to the break room and stripped off the coveralls that protected his clothes and washed his hands and face, getting as much of the grease smell off of him as he could.

He wasn't sure what had possessed him to invite her out to dinner. This whole fake boyfriend thing was fine if it was the only way to discourage somebody who just wouldn't take the hint that she wasn't interested, but that was about as far as he was willing to take it. And as soon as that dude backed off and turned his attention to someone else, which hopefully would be this Saturday, this fake relationship bullshit was over. Other than that, there was no reason for him to spend time and money on this woman.

Except that, whether he should or not, he fucking wanted to.

When he returned to the waiting room, everyone was gone except for Faye and Rocky, who were exactly as he'd left them. "Ready to go?"

Faye gave Rocky a pat on the head and stood, trying and failing to brush the fur from her black pants. "Yup."

"I have a thing in the truck that'll get that off." He started to take her hand, because holding her hand just seemed like the most natural thing in the world to do, but pulled back before their fingers touched, frowning at himself. "So where's this museum?" he asked as he held the door open for her and Rocky.

"Just down the street from the coffee shop. And I have my car. I can run by there and meet you at the restaurant. Where did you want to go?"

"Or you can just ride with me, and I'll bring you back to get your car later," he told her as they walked to his truck. What the hell? It wasn't like he was breaking any pack rules. He was just taking his fake girlfriend to dinner. Check that. Fake *fiancée*.

Yeah, they needed to talk about that.

Faye gave him a shy smile that seized his heart. "That'll work too. I live close to here."

"Oh yeah? Where?"

She glanced over at him, and he had the feeling she was weighing the risk of telling a practical stranger where she lived. But in the end, she decided to trust him. "I live at the RV park just up the road toward town."

Adam stopped as they reached the truck. "That's kinda out in the middle of nowhere." He didn't know that he liked the idea of her living out there by herself. "Do you live alone?"

This time, she just smiled and didn't answer him. "Are you going to unlock the truck so we can go get that dinner, or are we just gonna do our talkin' out here in the cold?"

Reaching up and grasping the door handle, he waited for the telltale beep and heard the locks, then he pulled the door open for her. "In the back, Rocky," he ordered when the wolf dog tried to follow her into the cab. With a huff, he did what he was told and went to the back to wait for Adam to lower the tailgate for him. Normally, he didn't like him riding back there. But this town was so small, there wasn't a road with a speed limit over 45 mph. And Rocky liked to ride in the back. Usually.

"There's a sticky roller in the glovebox," he told Faye. "To get my dog's fur off your clothes."

"Thanks." She found the roller and he closed her door, then walked around the back of the truck, opening the tailgate for Rocky and closing it behind him before going around to the driver's side.

Once she was de-furred and he had the heater going, she told him how to get to the museum. "Make a left here."

She pointed down 4th street. Adam did as he was told. "Pull a U-turn at the end of the road and then you can park anywhere along the road here." Again, he did as she directed. Then he put the truck in park and looked out his window at a bunch of old buildings that lined the road on the other side of a small fence. "All I see are a bunch of run-down buildings."

"Not just any run-down buildings," she told him. "There are forty-four authentic mining town buildings that are filled with thousands of artifacts and represent a mining town between 1860 and 1900."

"This was an old mining town?"

"Yup. Some of the buildings are on their original sites. But most of them were moved here from abandoned camps in the area." She paused and stared past me out the window. "It's not the kind of museum I've always dreamed of working in, but I like it."

"You wanted to work in a museum?"

"Yeah. It's always been my dream job. I'm working on my Master's degree in fine art."

Adam stared at her as the sun set over the horizon and the streetlights flickered on. There was more to this small-town girl than he knew.

"Anyway, I'll just be a minute." She opened the door and hopped out.

"Wait," he called. "I'll help you." Adam told Rocky to stay in the back of the truck and followed her around the fenced-in buildings to what looked like a storage building.

Faye pulled a set of keys out of her coat pocket and unlocked the padlock on the door. She put the keys back in her pocket and swung the door open. Inside, the room was temperature controlled at what felt to be about sixty-five degrees. She flicked on the lights, and Adam looked around at a room full of boxes and shelves filled with what appeared to be old artifacts. "What is all this?"

Faye followed his gaze. "It's a bunch of old things that we aren't using in the buildings right now. We swap them out every once in a while..." She let the sentence fall and turned to look at him. "Look, I'd like to explain what happened."

Adam crossed his arms over his chest as his eyes found her in the dimly lit room. She looked so contrite, it was all he could do not to close the distance between them and hold her and tell her everything was going to be okay. However, he knew if he did that, she'd never have the chance to explain herself with his mouth covering hers. And he really shouldn't do that. This fake relationship was exactly that—fake. And that's the way it needed to stay.

"I'd just finished up the morning rush at the coffee shop," she started. "When Jeff came in."

Immediately, Adam's skin began to crawl with the urge to shift. Dropping his arms, he took a step toward her and stopped. "What did he do?"

"Well, nothing really," she told him. "I mean, nothing physical, if that's what you mean. He just leaned over the counter and kept throwing questions at me."

Adam narrowed his eyes. "What kind of questions?"

"Questions about you. And me. And how we got together. He still doesn't believe we are. Together, I mean. And next thing I knew, I'd blurted out that we were engaged just to shut him up and get him out of there."

"Did it work?"

She nodded, and the tension slowly seeped from Adam's shoulders.

"I think all I did was piss him off, though." Then she sighed. "Anyway, I'm so sorry. He must've run off and blabbed to Margo, who, of course, told the entire town in record time." She paused again. "I don't know why I said something like that to him. I just panicked. But I'll fix it. Actually, I'm going to tell everyone that we're not really together at all. It's not fair of me to ask you to do something like this. You don't even know me."

No, but he'd really, really like to. "What about your unwanted admirer?"

She gave him a helpless look that tore at his chest. "I don't know what to do about him. But I'll deal with it. He's not your problem. He's mine." A self-depreciating smile played around her sweet lips. "I don't even know what I ever did to make him like this. I mean, I was always nice to him, but I try to be nice to everyone." Her eyes, when she looked up at him, were entreating. "I must've done *something*—"

Adam had heard enough. He closed the distance between them and grabbed her chin, forcing her to look at him. "Whatever's happened between you and this guy, it wasn't your fault, Faye. Some guys just don't know how to take no for an answer is all."

She gave him a grateful look, and rested the palms of her hands on his chest as he released her chin. He felt the heat of her touch all the way through his thermal shirt. "Thank you for saying that. But the truth of it is, you don't even know m—"

His mouth was on hers, her lips pliant and surprised beneath his own. Adam kissed her softly, carefully, cupping her face between his palms so she couldn't pull away. Her skin was as soft as silk beneath his fingertips. Tentatively, knowing he shouldn't, he tasted her, probing between her lips with his tongue until she opened for him and let him inside. A low growl rumbled through him as her fingers dug into his chest and her hands fisted his shirt, hanging on tightly. She tasted sweet and warm and innocent.

She tasted like HIS.

One hand moving to grip her soft hair, he wrapped his other arm around her and pulled her closer until her breasts pressed into his chest and his cock swelled against her stomach. His lungs rose and fell with harsh breaths, breathing in her scent, pulling it inside of him until there was nothing else but Faye. The smell of her, the taste of her...the *feel* of her.

Her arms wrapped around his neck, and Adam's wolf purred with pleasure, sensitizing his skin and warming his blood. He stepped forward, trying to bring her even closer. He wanted to feel her against him, skin to skin. Wanted to crawl inside of her until there were no barriers between them.

Faye stepped back as he moved forward until there was nowhere else for her to go and she was pressed against the shelf behind her. Adam ran his hands down her back and over the sweet curves of her hips, then hooked them beneath her thighs and lifted until her ass was on the edge of the shelf and her legs were wrapped his waist. He rolled his hips, growling deep when his rock-hard cock slid along her core.

Holy shit. He was about to come in his jeans.

Thank the gods they weren't his Brunello Cucinelli's.

CHAPTER 6

FAYE

Faye gazed off into the distance, not seeing the dirty window above the sink of her RV, the fingertips of one hand resting on her lips, and a persistent ache low in her belly as she remembered the way Adam had kissed her at the museum.

Her other hand was resting in a bowl of warm, sudsy dishwater, the dishes she was washing forgotten as she remembered the way the rough palms of his hands had seared her skin when he slid them beneath her shirt, his fingertips digging in as if he was afraid she would disappear, and a deep moan escaping his throat like he'd never felt anything better than her.

One thing was for sure, *she'd* never felt anything better than the way that man had kissed her. Her face was on fire—along with certain other parts of her—just thinking about it. She would've fucked him right there in the storage room, most happily, if he'd kept going.

Unfortunately, he hadn't. As soon as she'd slid her hands down his hard chest and grabbed the waistband of his jeans, he'd stiffened against her, his entire body freezing up hard as a board. With one last squeeze of his fingers, he'd broken off the kiss and backed away after carefully setting her back on her feet.

Then he'd apologized.

He'd fucking apologized.

Waving off his awkward words, Faye had turned away and tried to get herself together as she searched for the box of old newspaper clippings she'd been wanting to sort through ever since she'd first found it. He'd helped her carry it out to the truck, where Rocky was waiting patiently, and then she'd begged off dinner, claiming she'd forgotten she'd promised her mom she'd stop by.

The ride back to the garage where she'd left her car was... not comfortable. But like any woman who'd been kissed senseless one moment and then just as suddenly rejected, Faye thanked him and smiled so hard her cheeks hurt as he transferred the box to her car. Then she gave Rocky a warm goodbye with some head scritches and headed to her car. Adam remained standing beside his truck until she got in and started the engine. With one last smile and a little wave, she pulled away.

Just smile and wave, girl. Smile and wave.

She'd made it all the way to her driveway before that smile slipped and the tears began to fall.

Now it was Thursday, and Faye hadn't seen or heard from Adam since that night. She assumed this meant their date for Saturday was off.

Well, that was okay. It was unfair of her to drag him into her problems with Jeff. She'd go meet her friends alone and make an excuse for Adam. She'd tell them they'd had a fight. Something that would lead to their eventual "breakup."

She *would* just say they'd already split, but being engaged one minute and single the next would most certainly raise suspicions. She'd give it a week or two of them not getting along and then admit they'd rushed into things and called it quits.

Of course, she could always just admit that she'd faked the entire thing to get Jeff off her back. Faye thought about that for a second. The idea was tempting. Maybe it would finally get it through his thick skull that she didn't want to date him *so much* she was willing to lie about already being in a relationship.

But who was she kidding? He'd probably just turn it around and make it look like she'd done it to get his attention. And then she'd forever be known as the girl who was so pathetic she made shit up to get a guy's attention.

Sometimes living in a small town really sucked. If she lived in a big city, it would be easier to avoid people and she wouldn't be reduced to playing high school games.

With a heavy sigh, Faye went back to doing the dishes. She only had about an hour before she was supposed to pick up Jules for their regular Thursday girls' night out, which consisted of lots of wine in a corner booth of Greg's bar and many toasts to what they had, what they'd lost, and the amazing things they had coming, in between fits of giggles as they gossiped about the other people in town.

Wiping her hands on the dishtowel, Faye glanced at the clock and debated whether or not she should make a little effort with her appearance or just go out in the kitten leggings and gray sweatshirt she currently wore. She'd just decided to at least put on a bra and change her shirt since the one she was wearing now had big wet spots all over the front, when there was a knock on her door.

Frowning, Faye checked the time on her phone. Had she gotten the time wrong, and Jules had gotten tired of waiting for her?

But it wasn't Jules waiting impatiently on her doorstep.

"What are you doing here?" she blurted.

Adam stood at the bottom of the stairs, looking up at her. His green eyes started at the slippers on her feet and slowly roamed up her legs, paused at her hips with a flare of his nostrils, then continued up her oversized sweatshirt to her face, until finally taking in the mess of her hair thrown haphazardly on top of her head with a hair band. "I thought we could go on that real date before our fake one on Saturday. Have you eaten yet?"

The rough gravel of his voice sent chills chasing each other up and down her spine as she stared at him in confusion.

He cleared his throat. "So, is that what you're wearing?"

Faye frowned, completely thrown off kilter by his appearance at her door. "What?"

He nodded toward her kitten leggings.

She glanced down at herself, completely forgetting in that instant what she had on. "Oh. Uh. I've been home all day." They stared at each other until a gust of wind blew past, bringing some snow flurries with it. Faye shivered and blinked, breaking the spell. "I'm sorry. Come in. Please." She held the door open for him until he climbed the steps and stepped inside. Her breasts brushed against his chest as he squeezed by, and Faye sucked in a breath as her nipples hardened, keeping her eyes at the level of his collarbone.

Once he was in, she pulled the door closed and watched him as he looked around at her home. It wasn't much, but it was bought and paid for and, with the help of some friends, Faye had fixed it up until it was cozy and homey. She'd put in new flooring. Then she'd gotten rid of the dark cabinets and refaced them and made them white with new hardware. Behind the stove, she'd added some fun copper-washed white tiles in a floral design. Her fridge was small and white, as was her sink and stove. But it was a good-sized kitchen for her. She'd removed the extra cabinets on the other side to make more room for a table and a couch, painted the entire thing white, including the bathroom and her bedroom and added some accent wallpaper in more floral designs that reminded her of the wildflowers native to Colorado. The bedroom at the other end was mostly used as a giant closet with a large dresser and a small guest bed. She'd done it all herself, and she was very proud of the way it had turned out.

But still, she braced herself for his disgust. Faye could tell by the cut of his clothes that Adam came from money, something she'd never really had much of.

Adam turned back to her. "I like this. It's...you."

She listened for the lie and didn't hear it. "Me?"

He shrugged one shoulder. "Yeah. It feels like summer in here." Closing his eyes, he inhaled deeply. "And it smells like you."

What a weird thing to say. "Um, well, I live here. So..." Faye trailed off, her face too warm and her body entirely too aware of Adam standing in the middle of her small home.

He opened his eyes and, if she didn't know better, she would swear they were glowing.

"I guess I'll go get changed." She pointed over her shoulder with her thumb as she backed away toward her bedroom. She'd have to text Jules and reschedule. "I'll be right back." Turning swiftly away from the heat of his stare, she was almost to the safety of her room when he spoke.

"Faye, wait."

She stopped but didn't turn around.

"I'd like to say something first."

She glanced back over her shoulder. Adam was leaning casually against the counter with his big arms crossed over his hard chest. Faye remembered the feeling of that chest well. She fisted her hands at her sides, her palms tingling with the sudden urge to touch him again. Only maybe this time without the barrier of his shirt.

But she was being ridiculous. Adam wasn't interested in her that way. Or if he was, he didn't think she was worth going there. He'd made that abundantly clear the other day. Her shoulders fell as she turned to face him. "Look, I know what you're going to say. And you're right. This is stupid. This whole idea was stupid. And I'm really sorry I dragged you into it. But I still plan to tell everyone Saturday night that we're not really dating. That I made it all up." Saying it out loud made her realize it was the right thing to do. Even if the idea made her face and chest burn with embarrassment. "Honestly, I wasn't really expecting to hear from you again. So you don't have to take me out tonight or come with me Saturday. Although I do really appreciate that you kept your promise to take me."

He waited until she was done talking and stood there awkwardly, shifting from foot to foot as she waited for him to respond. "Actually, I wasn't going to say any of that," he told her. "And I don't know if telling your friends the truth is a good idea."

Faye frowned. "Why not?"

"Because if you do that, Jeff will think you lied to get his attention. I've known guys like that my whole life, and that's how they think. They're too full of themselves to entertain the idea that a woman could possibly just not be attracted to them."

Even though that was exactly what she'd been thinking, she released a soft, disparaging laugh. "Or it'll just make me look like a girl so desperate for a boyfriend that she bullies the first guy she sees into pretending he is."

"You didn't bully me. I offered. And I was glad to help."

That was true. He had.

Pushing himself away from the counter, Faye held her breath as he approached, stopping so close to her she was afraid to take a deep breath for fear he'd feel how hard her nipples were. This man did things to her. Things she'd never experienced before and didn't understand.

His fingertips skimmed her temple lightly as he brushed a few stray hairs away from her eye. "But like I said, that's not what I was going to say." He paused, his green eyes traveling over her face. "I wanted to apologize for the other night."

Faye's blood went cold, even as her skin still tingled from his nearness. She took a step back, putting some much-needed space between them. "You already did that, so it's really not necessary to do it again." *You already made me feel like a fool once, so please, please, don't say anything else.*

But he kept talking anyway. "I didn't mean for any of that to happen, and I didn't handle things very well, and I'm sorry," he told her. "I never wanted to make you feel embarrassed or anything."

"I wasn't—"

He interrupted her, talking fast, like he couldn't hold the words in any longer. "The truth is, I've had a hell of a time staying away from you these last few days."

Whatever she was about to say was forgotten. "W-what?"

Adam closed the distance between them again, pushing her back against the wall outside her bedroom until she had nowhere left to go and she felt like her heart was going to pound out of her chest. His eyes locked with hers until she couldn't look away. "You set my blood on fire." He shook his head slightly. "And I can't think of anything but the way you felt in my arms. How you tasted. How you would feel beneath me."

When she could bring herself to speak, her voice was little more than a whisper. "But, I thought..." Faye frowned, confused. "I thought...you said you were sorry." He'd acted appalled when she'd reached for his pants. He'd pulled away. And Faye had spent the last few days trying to convince herself, unsuccessfully, that it wasn't because he thought she was a slut who moved too fast. But she hadn't been able to help herself. The only thing she was able to think of when he'd kissed her like that was having him inside of her.

Ducking his head down to hers, Faye felt his warm breath near her ear. As though he read her mind, he said, "It wasn't anything you did. I loved having your hands on me. I just..."

She tried not to move. Or breathe. Or do anything that would keep him from saying whatever he was about to say. Because she desperately needed to know.

"I shouldn't be doing this with you."

Oh.

Her heart sank into her stomach. "Because you're already taken." Of course. Of course, he was. Just look at him. A guy who looked like that, and dressed the way he did, and who was nice enough to help out a woman who had an unwanted admirer. She didn't know why the thought had never occurred to her.

But his answer surprised her. "No. At least not the way you think."

Faye was so confused. His hard body—and she could feel exactly how hard he was *everywhere*—was telling her one thing, and his words another. "I don't understand."

He pulled back just enough to look her in the eye. "Neither do I." His eyes dropped to her lips, and Faye wet them with her tongue. She wanted to touch him so badly, but was afraid if she did, it would pull him out of whatever the hell this was and he'd leave again. So, instead, she kept her palms flush against the wall behind her.

When his lips finally pressed to hers, Faye swayed on her feet as her blood rushed through her body, making her lightheaded, her lungs aching from holding her breath. Breathing in through her nose, she was overwhelmed with his scent as it invaded her lungs. He pulled back until their lips were just barely touching, his soft and warm as they brushed hers.

"But I can't stop it."

ADAM

*H*e needed to stop.

He shouldn't be doing this.

Adam knew he was taking a huge risk, but he couldn't deny himself another taste of her. Just a taste. That's all he planned to take. At least until he heard the small whimper of need in the back of her throat and smelled the scent of her desire rising between them.

He growled low in response, every thought he had of only stealing a kiss lost as soon as her tongue touched his and her soft curves pressed perfectly against him. His instincts told him this woman was his, but an overwhelming sense of guilt tugged at his soul. It was dangerous to mess around with a human. Not only for him, but for the human if the rest of the pack found out. Riko had told him and Lex how they'd gone after Addison when they found out he still had feelings for her.

And if anything happened to Faye...

His arms slid around her and tightened, like he could keep her safe if he just held her tight enough. It wasn't just the threat to the pack if she found out who and what they were that concerned him. Wolves kept to their own. They normally didn't breed with humans. And there was a reason for that. Human women didn't survive the birth of a child conceived with a shifter. It was a well-known fact.

And yet, even knowing the risk he took by being with her, he couldn't bring himself to leave. Cupping the fragile bones of her jaw in one hand, he teased her with his lips and tongue until she opened for him. She tasted like warm honey. Like sunshine.

Like home.

He rolled his hips against her, instinctively trying to ease the ache to have her body wrapped tight around his cock, as his other hand found the bottom of her ridiculously large sweatshirt and the soft skin beneath. Deepening the kiss, he squeezed her waist before sliding his hand up over her ribcage until he felt the under curve of her breast. He paused, but only for a second, before, with a moan, he cupped her in his palm, brushing his thumb over her hard nipple. Her blood raced to meet his touch, heating her skin, and her heart pounded so hard he could hear it and feel its heavy beats beneath his fingers.

Faye's breath caught, and her hands flew to his shoulders and hung on tight.

"Too much?" he asked quietly, his lips a fraction of an inch from hers. He would stop if she wanted him to. It would kill him. But he would do it.

"Yes," she whispered. "No. Oh, god..." With a sound of surrender, she arched her back and pressed herself into his hand.

Adam pulled her sweatshirt up and off, dropping it on the floor as his hungry eyes roamed over her torso. Her skin was smooth, flawless, with light freckles on her shoulders from the sun, her breasts perfectly full enough to fill his hands. His mouth began to water as he imagined how her skin would taste and he started to kiss his way down her throat to her collarbone, her shoulder, the underside of her arm. His wolf pressed against his ribs, unable to stay still with so many emotions running through him, and he stilled for a moment as he fought the instinct to let him out.

"Please," Faye breathed. "Adam...please."

Growling low in his throat, he grabbed her by the back of the thighs and lifted her up the wall until her legs wrapped around his waist and those luscious breasts with their large, pink nipples were in his face. He sucked one into his mouth, ignoring the voice inside his head telling him to stop. To step away. To leave before things went too far and Faye was branded as his.

Because the truth of the matter was, it was way too fucking late for that. He'd known it the moment she came up beside him in the bar and asked for his help with those blue eyes of hers. The moment he'd smelled her scent and felt her in his arms on the dance floor.

Faye's head hit the wall behind her as she wrapped her bare arms around his head to hold him right where he was. Her chest rose and fell rapidly, small sounds of pleasure escaping her sweet mouth as he sucked and nipped and soothed first one nipple and then the other. His fingers dug into her thighs, his blood on fire.

So many thoughts and feelings spiraled inside of him. This was too fast. He barely knew her. She had no idea what he was or what she was getting herself into by being with him. But drowning it all out was the burning need to possess her. To make her his. To make her feel so good, she'd never want to be with anyone else. The instinct so strong the only thing that could stop him now was the woman moaning in his arms.

"Tell me to stop," he whispered desperately against her warm skin.

"I don't want you to stop," she told him. "Please, Adam. Don't stop."

Closing his eyes, he knew it was all over.

Sliding one arm under her ass and the other wrapped tight around her back, he pulled her away from the wall and walked with her into her bedroom, carefully laying her on the bed. Straightening, Adam kicked off his shoes, then reached behind him with one hand, grabbed his sweater, and yanked it over his head, dropping it on the floor beside his shoes.

Faye's eyes darkened as they traveled over him, much as he had her, taking in his shoulders, arms, and chest before dropping to his lean stomach. And lower. He liked that she wasn't shy. That she looked at him as hungrily as he had her.

She watched as he unfastened his jeans with shaking hands, his stomach tightening as his fingers brushed his swollen cock. The way she watched him...gods. He was about to come before he even got his pants off. But, somehow, he managed not to embarrass himself, removing the rest of his clothes as she lifted her hips and shimmied out of her kitten leggings. Her slippers fell to the floor as they joined his sweater.

When she lay there with nothing hiding her from him, Adam found, for a moment, that he couldn't move. He just drank in the sight of her. He'd never in his life seen a woman more perfectly made for him. "You're so fucking beautiful, Faye."

"So are you," she told him. There was a hint of surprise in her tone that made one corner of his mouth turn up.

She reached for him, and he lowered himself on top of her, careful not to crush her with his weight. Their mouths and bodies surged together like they'd done this a hundred times, her hips rising to meet his. He wanted to slow down, to take his time with her. He wanted to taste her come on his mouth and feel her come apart beneath his hands. But that would all have to wait. Right now, he just wanted—no, he *needed*—to be inside of her.

But he didn't have a condom.

He dropped his head with a curse. "Fuck!"

"What's wrong?" Her eyes were wide and worried as she stared up at him.

"I don't have anything," he gritted out. "I don't have a condom." He wasn't worried about diseases. He couldn't catch or transmit anything like that. But he would *not* take the chance of getting her pregnant. With a groan, he sank his teeth into the muscle between her neck and shoulder.

Faye winced at the pain, but her nails dug into his back and her hips rose from the bed. Adam moaned as his cock slid along her thigh. "I don't care," she told him. "Probably stupid of me, but I don't."

"I can't take a chance you'll get pregnant." Adam kissed the bite mark he'd left on her skin. "You barely know me," he added as an excuse.

"I won't," she told him. "I have an implant. It's good for another two years." Lifting her arm, she stretched it out until he could see the small but unmistakable rod just under her skin.

That's all he needed to fucking know.

Hunger flared within him, and he hooked one arm beneath her knee and lifted her leg, opening her to him. With one surge, he was halfway inside, Faye's lusty cry of surprise ringing in his ears. She was wet, but she was tight, her body hugging him when he withdrew until his eyes nearly rolled back in his head. Another push, and he was balls deep inside of her, swallowing her cries as his mouth covered hers.

He kissed her mindlessly, his body taking over as the blood rushed from his head, sensitizing his skin until every slide of skin on skin sent a rush of desire straight to his cock. Hips pumping, Adam cried out as he came so hard, he felt it all the way out to his fingers and toes.

Pulling out, he slid down her body and spread her legs wide. Her pink pussy was glistening with her desire and his, her clit swollen and begging to be touched. Adam lowered his mouth to her sex, tasting himself as well as her as he ran his tongue through her lips until he found her clit. With a moan, he sucked it into his mouth and flicked his tongue over the sensitive nub until Faye was writhing beneath him, her fingers tangled in his hair and soft moans and cries coming from her mouth. A few seconds later, she arched, her hips rising and her body tensing, her hands holding his head where it was before she cried his name and bucked beneath him.

Adam rode out her orgasm, slowing only when she collapsed to the bed, breathless. Running his tongue over her, he drank her in, and she was even sweeter than he'd imagined.

Rising to his knees, he rolled her over, lifted her hips so her perfectly round ass was in the air, and drove back inside of her. Faye fisted the comforter, pushing her sweet ass back to meet him thrust for thrust as he told her how gorgeous she was. How perfect. And how crazy she made him.

Minutes or hours later, when she was limp as a doll in his arms and he could finally breathe, he laid down on the bed and pulled her against him so her back was to his front. Holding her tight, listening to her heart fall back into a normal rhythm as her eyes closed and her breathing slowed, Adam felt the weight of what he'd done sink into him.

He was going to have to talk to Riko. See if maybe since he and Addison were a thing now, the rules could be relaxed a bit. Then he would have to talk to Faye. Tell her what he was, and hope to hell she didn't freak out.

Because she was his now.

And his she would stay.

CHAPTER 8

ADAM

The next day, Adam caught Riko as he came into the garage. "Hey, can I talk to you for a sec?"

Riko studied him for a second, his expression giving nothing away, before saying, "Sure. Let's go into the break room."

Adam closed the door behind them. "I need to talk to you about Faye. The girl I met on New Year's."

Riko held up one hand, palm out, stopping the speech Adam had practiced all morning before he even had a chance to say anything. "I know what you're about to say. I can smell her all over you."

Adam didn't try to deny it, but he could tell from Riko's tone this wasn't going to be an easy discussion. His jaw clenched as he lifted his chin. "I can't give her up, so please don't ask me to."

"You barely know her."

"I want the chance to get to do that."

They stared each other down for a few seconds before Adam lowered his eyes and bowed his head in deference to his alpha.

"You know the pack laws," Riko said. "You know how inflexible they are here, Adam. I've already had to shut down two attempts to banish you from the pack. And you know damn well this won't be the last of it. What in the hell were you thinking?"

"Probably the same thing you were when you came back for Addison. A pure human, I might add."

"I didn't come back for her. I came back to bury my father and things just...happened. Besides, it's different with me and Addi. I've known her for a lot of years. And we had a thing going back in the day." He sighed. "Look, I know I'm being a damn hypocrite right now. But you know what happened the minute the rest of the pack caught a whiff of what was going on between us. They were ready to take her out to protect themselves. And that was with me."

Adam knew what he was trying to say. Riko was a dominant wolf. An alpha. And they were still willing to risk his wrath to remove the chance that Addison would tell the world about their existence.

"You're putting that girl's life in danger, man." He studied Adam's face. "And what happens if she gets pregnant?"

"That won't happen."

"It might."

"It won't."

"Have you even asked her if she wants kids? Is she okay with never having any?"

Scrubbing his face with his palms, Adam paced away. He didn't know. He had no fucking idea what Faye wanted or didn't want. "I don't know," he finally admitted.

"How do you not know?" Riko asked him. "I hear y'all are engaged."

Adam barked out a laugh. "Small town rumors that got out of hand to keep away an unwanted admirer. That's all."

Gesturing for Adam to sit down at one of the round lunch tables, Riko took the seat across from him, crossing his arms on the tabletop as he leaned forward and speared Adam with his sharp gaze. "Look, I'm just trying to think of Faye here. I wouldn't want anything to happen to her.

And I can't guarantee that with the way things are with the pack right now."

"You're the alpha now," Adam reminded him. "They'll do what you tell them."

Riko laughed. "And you're a goddamn idiot if you believe that. This pack, although it's getting better, is still too fucking volatile for me to trust any of them. And I'm not completely convinced a few of the rowdier ones aren't meeting behind my back, trying to think of a way to get rid of me, without dying, that the rest of the pack will accept."

Adam knew exactly the wolves he was talking about. "They'll never get enough support from the rest of the pack. And if they try, Lex and I will be there to make sure you kick their asses fair and square."

"I appreciate that," Riko told him.

Adam played with a saltshaker someone had left on the table. "I can't let her go, Riko."

"Why not?"

"Because she's *mine*. I knew it the first moment I saw her."

Their gazes clashed.

"Are you really gonna tell me I have to stay away from her?"

Riko sighed heavily. "No, man. I'm not gonna tell you that. I mean, hell. What's the point now? The entire fucking town already thinks you two are planning the happy nuptials."

"Thank you, Riko."

Riko waved away his thanks. "Yeah, yeah. Just keep a close eye on her until we can make sure no one is going to come after her." His head snapped up, and he pointed a finger at Adam. "And even if you decide she's not worth it, it's still your responsibility to keep her safe. I don't give a shit if you're stuck in this town the rest of her life. Understood?"

Adam tried to contain the grin that was spreading across his face, but couldn't do it. "Understood. And thank you."

"And I'm not helping you when the pack comes after you."

"Yes, you will."

Giving him a "fuck you" look, Riko told him, "You're right. I will. But seriously, Adam. I'm not happy that you're putting me in this position when they're just starting to simmer down about me and Addi."

"I know. And I'm sorry. I owe you one."

"Hell yeah, you do. Now get your ass to work."

The rest of the day was busy. It seemed everyone in town who owned a car got together and decided this was the day to get it repaired or tuned up for the year. There was no way they'd get them all finished, but Adam got as much done as he could until his stomach told him it was time to call it quits and go get something to eat. Preferably between Faye's legs.

"Steve! I'm heading out," he called to the one other guy who'd stayed late. "You good to lock up?"

"Yeah, I got it. I'm just double checking this hose, and I'll be right behind you."

"See you tomorrow. Let's go, Rocky." Adam hung up the customer's keys and stripped out of his coveralls, then grabbed what was left of his lunch from the break room before checking the front door was locked and leaving through the back door.

He just wanted to run by his place and get a quick shower and some food for Rocky. Pulling out his phone, he texted Faye.

Up for some company?

Her response was nearly immediate.

Only if you're bringing pizza. :)

Adam grinned.

That I can do. What kind do you like?

He got her order and started the truck.

Thirty minutes later, he was smelling a lot better and loading Rocky back into the truck with his dinner dish and dog food. He'd already called in the pizza order to Millonzi's and just had to swing by and pick it up on his way to Faye's. He'd also brought an overnight bag. It might be presumptuous of him, but Adam didn't plan on leaving her alone much until he was sure the pack wasn't going to come after her. So she was just going to have to get used to his company. And he was bringing Rocky to soften the blow.

By the time he got to Faye's RV, it had been a good hour since he'd texted her. Pulling up alongside her car, he noticed another truck parked up along the back end.

His hackles rose on the back of his neck when Rocky growled from the bed of the truck. Something was wrong.

Leaving the pizza in the truck, Adam ordered Rocky to stay where he was and jogged up to Faye's door. He could hear noises coming from inside, and his heart rose into his throat. "Faye!"

The door was locked when he tried it, but the sound of something smashing to the floor spurred him into action.

With a low growl, he yanked the door open, breaking the lock in the process. He was expecting to find one or more of the pack in there and he was terrified that they'd hurt her, that he'd gotten there too late, so he was already beginning to shift when he stormed inside.

What he hadn't expected to find was Jeff's large body on top of Faye's. He had her pinned to the couch, one hand over her mouth and the other tearing open her red flannel shirt, exposing her bare breasts as she pummeled him with her fists and tried to buck him off, her screams muffled by his large hand.

Her blue eyes were huge and terrified as they found his.

With a roar of rage, Adam shifted, the change coming on so hard and fast, he barely felt the pain. He crossed the small space with one push of his powerful back legs, jaws snapping as he threw himself into Jeff, knocking him off of Faye and into the table behind him, which broke and crumbled to the floor with their combined weight.

Jeff bared his teeth, his dark eyes flashing yellow. Adam narrowed his eyes. There was no fucking way he just saw what he thought he just saw. And yet, he didn't seem all that surprised to have a giant wolf on top of him.

But that was impossible. Adam could scent another shifter half a mile away. And this guy smelled human. Like an angry human, but human, nonetheless.

"You can't keep me away from her," he spit in Adam's face. "Faye was mine long before you ever came along. And she'll be mine again as soon as I take you out of the equation."

Adam snarled. The fuck he would. A human was no match for a shifter.

Shock shot through him as the bones in Jeff's face shifted beneath his skin, and at first, Adam thought it was just a trick of the light. But no, it wasn't. Jeff bared his teeth, the supernatural light behind his eyes sputtering to life again, stronger this time. His hands, pressed against Adam's chest in an attempt to keep his jaws away from his throat, elongated.

Just then, another section of the table gave way, sending them both tumbling to the floor. Adam slammed into the cabinets and quickly scrambled to his feet, ready to launch himself at this asshole again. But he stopped and watched as something he'd never seen happen before took place right before his eyes.

Falling to his hands and knees, Jeff's back con-caved and then arched, his shifting bones and muscles stretching his skin to the point that it should have torn open and healed again in a new form. Except it didn't. It stopped there.

Half changed, Jeff rose to his full height. He appeared to have grown an inch or two, and he was bigger, bulkier, the bones in his cheeks and jaw more prominent. He bared his teeth, and Adam saw they'd grown too.

Son of a bitch.

He glanced over at Faye. She'd pulled herself into a ball on the corner of the couch and now sat watching them, the scent of her fear sour and tears flowing down her cheeks. He needed to move this fight somewhere else, where she wouldn't get hurt.

Turning, Adam ran back outside through the broken door, heading east to the open land near Faye's RV park. Jeff—half shifted—followed right on his heels. Fire burned across Adam's back, Jeff's claws ripping right through his clothes to the skin beneath. Adam cursed, and decided they'd gone far enough. He skidded to a halt, turning to face the threat behind him.

Jeff hit him with the force of a freight train, his jaws open and going for his throat. But Adam knocked him away and followed him to the ground.

Snarls and snapping teeth ripped through the night air as they fought. And this wasn't just a fight for dominance. Adam was fighting for his life. The winner would get the girl. He had no time to wonder why he hadn't known what Jeff was. Or how he could only shift halfway. He was too busy trying to stay out of reach of Jeff's longer arm span. In this form, the guy was freaky strong. Stronger than Adam even. He couldn't let him get his arms around him, because he was pretty sure the guy would be able to crush his internal organs with one good squeeze.

And if that happened, no one would be around to protect Faye. He would do what he had to do to protect her and everyone else in this town. And worry about the consequences later.

And then, out of the corner of his eye, Adam saw a flash of steel in the moonlight.

Son of a bitch.

CHAPTER 9

FAYE

Faye sat on the couch with her arms wrapped around her knees, staring out the open door.

There was no way in hell she'd just seen what she thought she had.

No fucking way.

Because if she had, then she'd just watched the man who'd spent the night before in her bed turn from a man to a wolf between one blink and the next. And then she'd seen the man who'd coerced his way into her home under the guise of apologizing for his behavior of late and then attacked her, a man she'd known most of her life, change halfway into the same animal.

No. There's no fucking way she'd just seen that.

There was a noise at the door, and Faye jumped when she saw a large white head poke inside and look around. Spotting her, it came inside with a soft whine and eased up beside her.

Rocky. It was just Rocky.

He planted himself in front of her and growled in the direction of the door.

She didn't know how long they sat there like that, but eventually, she got herself together enough to try to button her shirt. However, most of the buttons had broken off, so she grabbed the ends of the shirt and tied it together. At least it kept her covered.

Rocky only looked over his shoulder at her and then sat down, his eyes going back to the door.

"Are you one of those things, too?" she asked him.

This time, he didn't even glance at her. He was too hyper-focused on his guard duties.

She should get up and see if she could close the door, but Faye was frozen to her spot on the couch.

Minutes or maybe hours later, she honestly couldn't have said, Rocky whined and stood up. Faye straightened too, her eyes going to the door.

A very bloody, and very naked, Adam appeared at the top of her steps. One arm was wrapped around his torso and his eyes were wild as they flew around the room, searching for her. As soon as he spotted her on the couch with Rocky standing guard, he moaned and fell to the floor.

Faye jumped off the couch and ran to him, the bewilderment and fear she'd felt just seconds before diminishing at the sight of him wounded and passed out on her floor.

Faye fell to her knees beside him and grabbed his shoulders. "Adam?"

"Adam!" she called again. His skin was way too pale, and there were beads of sweat dripping down his temple. She tried to see where all of the blood was coming from, but she was afraid to touch him anywhere. Her throat thick with tears, she said, "Hold on, Adam. Just hold on. I'm calling an ambulance."

His hand shot out and grabbed her wrist, scaring her. "No." His voice was raw. "No ambulance."

"I have to call," she told him. "I can't get you to a hospital by myself."

"No doctors," he insisted.

"You'll die if I don't get you to a hospital!"

"I won't," he told her. "I won't."

Faye crouched beside him, undecided. He was bleeding out all over her floor. How could he possibly think he'd be fine? She tried to tug her wrist out of his grip, but he was stronger than she expected for someone in his condition. Finally, she dropped back down to her knees beside him and took his face in her palms. There was some swelling and redness on his jaw and near his eye and mouth, but nothing looked broken. "Adam, please. Let me help you. I can't just sit here and let you die on my floor."

A small smile turned up one corner of his mouth. "I won't die. I promise." Then he turned his head and kissed the inside of her thumb. "I'm sorry I scared you."

"Why won't you let me help you?" she cried.

His green eyes were tight with pain, but clear, when they shot to hers. He reached out for her with his free hand. "Faye, I need to tell you about what just happened."

"The only thing I want to hear coming out of your mouth is that you're going to let go of me and let me go get my phone." That she'd left in her bedroom. *Dammit.*

"No phone. No ambulance. No doctors. I'll heal on my own."

"But there's so much blood..."

"I'll heal on my own," he told her again.

Sitting back, she twisted around and grabbed the towel that was hanging from the dishwasher, then started trying to clean him up enough to see where the worst of the bleeding was coming from. He had multiple wounds on his stomach, like he'd been stabbed with a wide knife. "Are these knife wounds?" she asked.

"Yeah, but that's not important." He winced as she pressed on the wounds as best she could. "Faye, honey, please stop and listen to me." Placing his hand over hers, he stopped her frantic movements. "I will heal, and I'll heal quick. I just need an hour or two."

She frowned down at him. "What the hell are you talking about? You won't. You need a doctor. You probably have internal damage."

"Probably. But that'll heal too."

"You're wrong, Adam. I think you're hurt worse than you think."

"Faye, I'm a shifter. I'll heal."

She heard the words, but she was so caught up in keeping the idiot alive that they didn't register at first.

"Faye." His voice was stronger, more insistent. His grip stronger. "Faye!"

He finally cut through the state of panic. Her eyes flashed up to his face.

"I'm a shifter," he repeated. "What you just saw. I'm a shifter. I'll heal. I'm not going to die."

"I don't understand." And she didn't. It all felt like some kind of weird dream.

He struggled to sit up more, and she quickly reached out to help him. Between the two of them, they managed to get him propped up against the cabinets. Rocky whined again and started licking his face. "It's okay, boy. I'm okay." His eyes found hers. "I'm sorry. This isn't the way I wanted to tell you."

"I know what I saw," she whispered. "But I feel like I'm going crazy. Am I going crazy?"

"No, honey. You're not crazy. You saw exactly what you saw. I'm a man who shifts into a wolf."

She barely managed to keep from laughing hysterically in his face. "But that's not possible," she told him uneasily. Because she knew he wasn't joking at all. She'd seen it with her own eyes. She'd watched him go from a man to a wolf, and now he was a man again.

And he was bleeding to death in her house.

"I'm not going to bleed to death." He smiled as she gave him a look that told him she didn't quite believe him. Had she said that out loud? "I'm a shifter, Faye. And I'm not the only one in this town."

"Why don't we get you to a doctor?" she suggested shakily. "And then you can tell me more about how you howl at the full moon, huh?"

"Why don't you lift that towel and see for yourself?" He nodded to where she was still pressing the towel to the worst of his wounds on his stomach. "Go ahead."

"I can't. I have to try to stop the bleeding."

"Faye."

Something in his tone had her raising her eyes to his.

"Just look." Placing his hand on top of one of hers, he helped her lift the towel.

Faye begged him with her eyes not to make her do it. She knew without a doubt that as soon as she lifted the towel away, he was going to bleed out and die right there on her kitchen floor. And then she would have to sell her RV that she'd worked so hard to make into her home because there was no way in hell she'd be able to keep living there.

"Faye, look."

She shook her head, her eyes glued to her face. "No. I can't."

"Honey. Look."

Reluctantly, she dropped her eyes down to his stomach. At first, she couldn't quite comprehend what she was seeing. "How is this possible?" The open gashes that were bleeding so profusely just a few minutes before were slowly but surely fusing back together. Some of the shallower ones looked like wounds that had happened weeks before and were already shiny scars. "What the hell is happening?" As she watched, the skin on either side of the worst wound pulled together. Like invisible fingers pressed on either side so an invisible needle could stitch it closed.

Adam didn't say anything, except to groan when she reached out to touch his newly healed skin. She pulled her hand back, afraid she'd hurt him. "I'm sorry."

"Don't be," he told her. "I love the way it feels when you touch me."

Flashes of the night before flew through her head, heating her blood despite the crazy things she was hearing and seeing. But the more she thought about it, the more there were things—just little things—that she hadn't really thought about, but which made sense now. Like the way he could lift her like she weighed next to nothing. Not to mention his stamina. Faye hadn't been with many men, but she'd heard enough stories from her friends to know that most of them were usually snoring the night away after one orgasm. Maybe two if they were younger. And yet Adam had woken her up throughout the night, taking her over and over again until the sun came up over the horizon and he'd had to leave for work, leaving her to get a few hours of sleep until she had to go to the coffee shop for the afternoon shift. "This isn't possible."

"It is. And I am." He paused. "I'll explain it all to you. I promise. But right now, I just need you to promise that you won't say anything about this to anyone. And I mean *no one*."

"Why not?"

"Because the livelihood of my pack depends on it. And so does your safety."

"Your pack?" There was a pack of...what did he call himself? Shifters?...living here in her town?

"Faye." He waited until she'd raised bewildered eyes up to his. "I need you to promise. Swear you won't say anything, just for now, until I can explain everything to you."

Her brain was short-circuiting. Or at least that's what it felt like. And her heart was racing, a burst of adrenaline rushing through her bloodstream, invoking her flight-or-fight response.

Faye chose flight.

She didn't know what the hell was going on, or if what she thought she'd just seen was true or not. But she knew what she was seeing right in front of her eyes now. Adam was healed enough now that he was pushing himself into more of a sitting position, every muscle rippling with renewed strength. And she needed to get out of there before he was fully recovered.

Pushing herself to her feet, she slipped in the drying blood and caught herself on the counter.

"Whoa...easy there," Adam told her. He was on his knees beside her, hanging onto her thighs to keep her upright. She hadn't even seen him move.

"I'm just going to grab some more towels," she told him. "To clean up the floor. And for you, if you want one."

His eyes narrowed. "Faye. Talk to me."

"I just need to get towels." Before he could stop her, she turned and slipped out the door and closed it behind her. Then she ran, her feet cold in her wet socks, heading for her car. She didn't know where she was going, but she had to get out of there. Go somewhere public. Somewhere he couldn't hurt her.

Strong arms wrapped around her, pulling her back inside and shutting the door. "Don't run. Please, don't run."

CHAPTER 10

ADAM

"Y̲ou're right," she told him. Her voice was shaking. "This is *my* house. YOU go."

Dammit. He was scaring her. "Faye, I swear I won't hurt you. I just want to talk. Please, just give me a chance. Then, if you want, I'll help you clean up and I'll go." When she didn't say anything, he told her, "I swear to you, you're safe with me. I was the guy you came to for help, remember?"

She was still tense in his arms, but after a moment, she nodded. "Okay."

"Okay?"

She nodded again.

"Okay. I've got some clothes in my truck."

"I can go get them for you."

The chance of her getting his clothes or hopping into his truck and taking off with his overnight bag and his dinner was about fifty-fifty. Maybe forty-sixty. But he didn't really have much of a choice. It was a miracle none of the neighbors had called the cops yet as it was. Luckily, the RVs at this park were pretty spread out this time of year.

Slowly, even though it was the last thing he wanted to do, he released her. "The doors are open."

"What about...Jeff?"

"He ran off. And I don't think he's coming back. But if he did, I'd know."

She didn't ask him how he would know. With a quick glance back at him over her shoulder, she slowly walked down the steps. He watched her go to the passenger side of his truck, open the door, and pull out his bag. After a brief hesitation, she grabbed the pizza boxes too, then shut the door by pushing it closed with her shoulder and brought everything inside.

Adam took the bag from her. He was still a little sore in the gut, but it looked like everything had stopped bleeding.

"You can shower if you want," she told him.

"Are you still going to be here when I get out?"

She looked over at the pizza, then back at him. "Well, I'm starving. So, yeah."

Reaching out, he cupped her face in his hand. "Are you okay? Did he hurt you?" Adam's entire body was tense as he waited for her answer.

"No," she told him. "Other than throwing me around a little, he didn't hurt me."

The tension left him, and he closed his eyes in relief.

"Thank you," she said quietly. "For helping me."

"You don't have to thank me," he told her. "I'm sorry I wasn't here sooner."

She gave him a small smile. "Go shower. You're bleeding all over my floor."

He started to turn away. "Hey, Faye?"

Her blue eyes rose to meet his.

"I'm still the same guy you met on New Year's. Nothing's changed there."

She stared at him for a long moment. "I know."

"Okay. Good." His eyes traveled over her face. She was calmer. The sour scent of fear gone. "I'll be right back."

When he came out, wearing a clean pair of jeans and a couple of bandages over the deepest of the wounds, he found her sitting on the couch, sharing her pizza crust with Rocky. On the cushion beside her was another plate with two slices on it.

"There's wine on the counter," she told him.

Adam found the two glasses of red and brought them over. "I'm sorry about your table. I'll replace it for you tomorrow."

"You'd better."

Sitting down beside her, he told Rocky to go lay down by the front door he'd managed to close but couldn't lock, then he handed her a glass of wine. "So what do you want to know?"

"Everything would be nice."

He smiled. "Okay. Um. So, my people have been around for a long time. As long as humans."

"You're not human?" To her credit, her voice was pretty steady as she asked the question.

"Not completely, no. But how that happened is a long story that I don't really want to get into right now. Suffice it to say, we're here. And we've lived among you for a long time."

Faye set her plate on the kitchen counter and then came back to the couch with her wine, sitting down and curling her legs beneath her. He noticed she'd changed too while he was in the shower, and was wearing a pair of gray sweatpants and a maroon T-shirt. She looked adorable.

The only thing that would make that outfit better was if it was his pants and his shirt she was wearing.

"And you can just...turn into a wolf?"

He nodded. "Yeah. You can call it magic. Or the supernatural. Or a fucked-up gene pool. But I've been able to do it ever since I hit puberty."

She was quiet for a moment. "Does it hurt?"

She voiced the question so softly and with so much concern in her voice, it made him set his plate on one of the kitchen chairs beside him that made it through the destruction. "Yeah. Sometimes worse than others."

"Can you control it? The change?"

"Most of the time."

Her brows lowered in concern. "Most of the time?" she repeated. Although she didn't change her expression, there was a change in her scent as she thought about that. A wisp of fear.

He turned more fully toward her. "Faye, I told you that I would never hurt you. And I meant it. You have nothing to fear from me. EVER."

"But, what if—"

"EVER," he told her. "Even if I shifted right now and no one else was here, I wouldn't hurt you."

"How do you know that?"

"Because I'm still me when it happens."

She got quiet again.

"Tell me what you're thinking."

Her bottom lip was between her teeth, and he reached up and touched her face, running his thumb over the plump flesh before pulling it out and smoothing his thumb over the bite.

"This is a lot to take in," she whispered. "I still feel like I'm going a little bit crazy."

"You're not crazy," he told her.

He was still touching her face. "I want to touch you."

"You are touching me."

One side of his mouth turned up. "And you're not screaming in terror."

She shook her head. "No."

"I want to touch you more."

Her breath quickened and her nostrils flared slightly. That earthy smell that was all her grew stronger, teasing his nose and igniting his blood. His cock was painfully hard now.

"You were just bleeding all over my floor," she argued. "You're still too pale."

"I've got enough blood left to handle making you feel good."

"I don't know what to say," she told him. "Or what to think. Or how to feel."

"Faye, I'm just asking for a chance here. That's all. I want to get to know everything about you. What you like. What you don't like. Your favorite thing to eat when you're home alone watching chick flicks. What you sing in the shower." He took her hands in his. "I shared my biggest secrets with you. I'd really love the chance to get to know yours."

"I don't have any secrets."

"We all have secrets. Some are just a little stranger than others." He smiled at her, and after a moment, she smiled back. "I'd like the chance to prove to you I can be a real boyfriend. And maybe someday, in the not so far future, a real fiancé." As soon as he said the words out loud, Adam knew in his gut that this would happen. Faye was his. And he was hers. All he needed was the time to prove it to her. "So, what do you say?"

"This is all just...I can't wrap my head around it."

"I know," he told her. "It's a lot. *I'm* a lot. But I swear, other than the fact that, occasionally, I'm as furry as Rocky over there, I'm just a guy. Who's head over heels crazy for you. Is it all one sided?"

She shook her head. "No, it's not one sided. I just..."

He waited for her to say more, and when she didn't, he made her an offer. "How about this? Tonight, we'll eat pizza, and drink wine, and maybe watch a crappy movie. Then tomorrow, we'll go pick you out a new table. If you want to talk, we'll talk. If you don't want to talk, we won't." His eyes roamed over her face. "A chance, Faye. That's all I'm asking for."

She stared at him for a long time, and he could practically hear the wheels turning in her head. But then, she surprised him again. "Okay," she told him.

He lifted his eyebrows. "Okay? Really?"

She smiled. "Yeah. Okay. But I don't want to watch a movie."

"What do you want to do?"

"I want to talk," she told him. "In bed."

Adam grinned. "Whatever my lady wants." His heart pounded in his chest. Somehow, he was going to convince this woman to be his one and only.

And if he had to keep her naked the entire time to do it...

Well, that was a sacrifice he was willing to make.

L.E. Wilson writes romance starring intense alpha males and the women who are fearless enough to tame them — for the most part anyway. ;) In her novels you'll find smoking hot scenes, a touch of suspense, some humor, a bit of gore, and multifaceted characters, all working together to combine her lifelong obsession with the paranormal and her love of romance.

Her writing career came about the usual way: on a dare from her loving husband. Little did she know just one casual suggestion would open a box of worms (or words as the case may be) that would forever change her life.

Lattes and music are a necessary part of her writing process, though sometimes you'll find her typing away at her favorite Starbucks. She walks two miles to get there, to make up for all of those coffees.

On a Personal Note:

"I love to hear from my readers! Contact me anytime at le@lewilsonauthor.com."

Keep In Touch With L.E.
lewilsonauthor.com
le@lewilsonauthor.com

facebook.com/LEWilsonAuthor

instagram.com/LEWilsonAuthor

bookbub.com/authors/l-e-wilson

tiktok.com/@LEWilsonAuthor